WONDER WOMAN
IS RESPECTFUL

Written by
CHRISTOPHER HARBO

Illustrated by
OTIS FRAMPTON

WONDER WOMAN created by
William Moulton Marston

Capstone Young Readers
a capstone imprint

Wonder Woman is respectful. She uses kind words and cares about other people's feelings. She treats others the way she likes to be treated herself.

When Wonder Woman asks for help, she remembers to say please.

Wonder Woman respects her friends by being polite.

When Wonder Woman receives a gift, she always says thank you.

The Amazon warrior shows respect by being grateful.

When Wonder Woman enters a building, she always holds the door.

Wonder Woman shows respect by putting others ahead of herself.

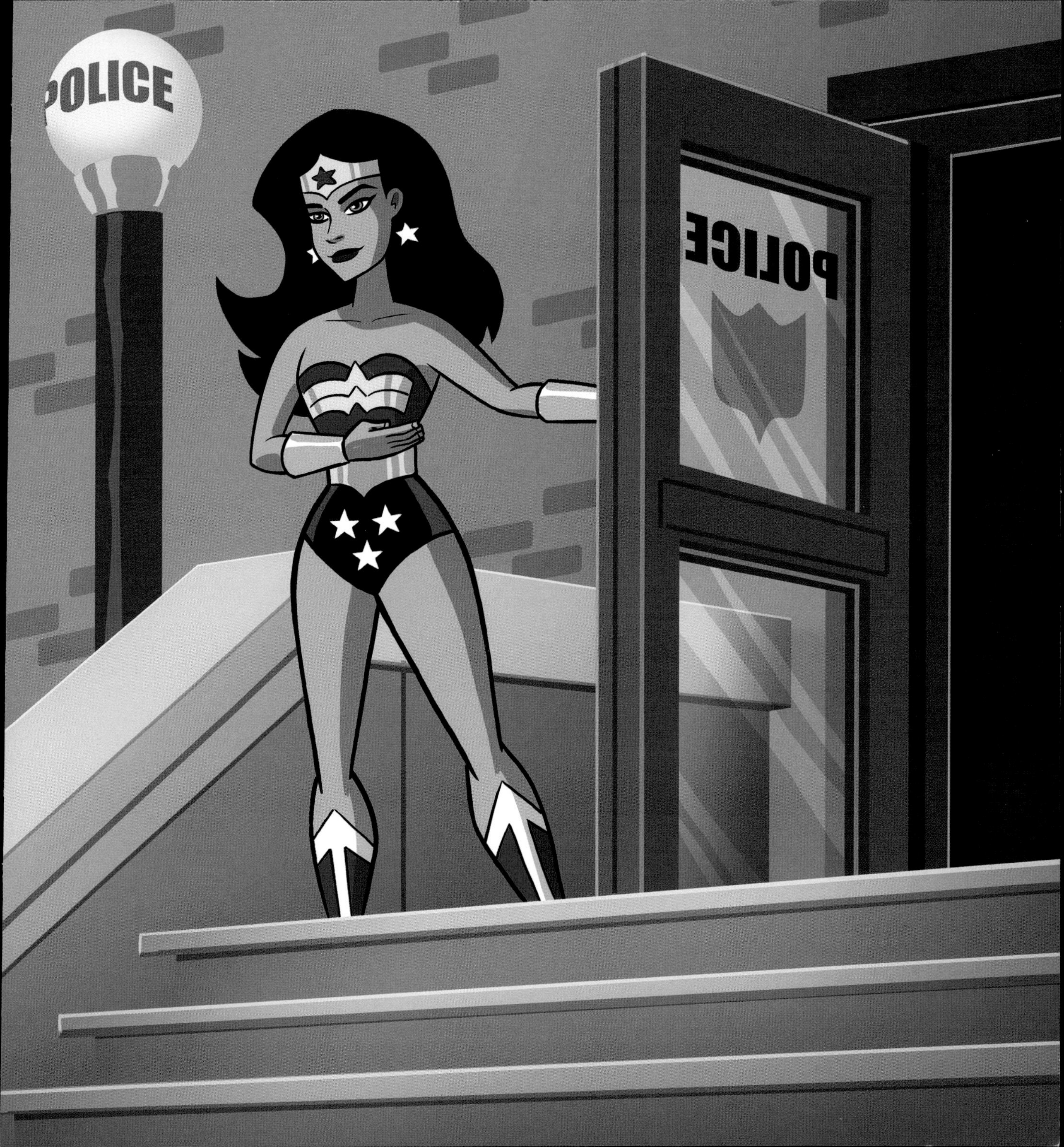
POLICE
POLICE

When Wonder Woman helps with a disagreement, she carefully listens to both sides.

The Amazon warrior respects different opinions and weighs them equally.

When Wonder Woman stops a crime,
she looks for a peaceful solution.

Wonder Woman respects the safety
of everyone — even her enemies.

When Wonder Woman meets new people,
she learns about their differences.

Wonder Woman shows respect by getting to know people better.

When Wonder Woman works on a team, she welcomes everyone's ideas.

The Amazon warrior respects other people's talents.

No matter what, Wonder Woman treats others the way she wants to be treated.

Wonder Woman shows respect by remembering that everyone needs help, even her enemies.

Even when super-villains need wrangling,
Wonder Woman treats them with respect.

And like it or not . . . they must respect her power.

WONDER WOMAN SAYS...

- Being respectful means using good manners, like when I say please to ask for Superman's help.

- Being respectful means you treat others the way you'd want to be treated, like when I help my enemy, Morgaine le Fey, when she is in danger.

- Being respectful means calmly solving problems, like when I help Batman and Green Lantern settle an argument.

- Being respectful means you welcome other people's ideas, like when I work with Batgirl, Supergirl, and Hawkgirl to capture Giganta.

- Being respectful means being the best you that you can be!

BE YOUR BEST
with the World's Greatest Super Heroes!

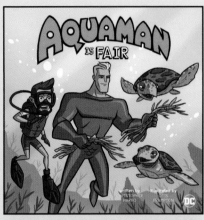

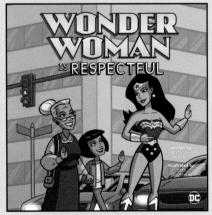

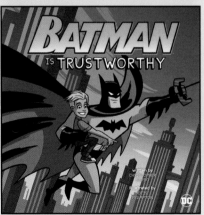

ONLY FROM CAPSTONE!

DC Super Heroes Character Education
is published by Capstone Young Readers
A Capstone Imprint
1710 Roe Crest Drive
North Mankato, Minnesota 56003
www.mycapstone.com

Editor: Julie Gassman
Designer: Hilary Wacholz
Art Director: Bob Lentz

Cataloging-in-Publication Data is available
at the Library of Congress website.

ISBN: 978-1-62370-957-0

Printed and bound in the USA.
112018   000054